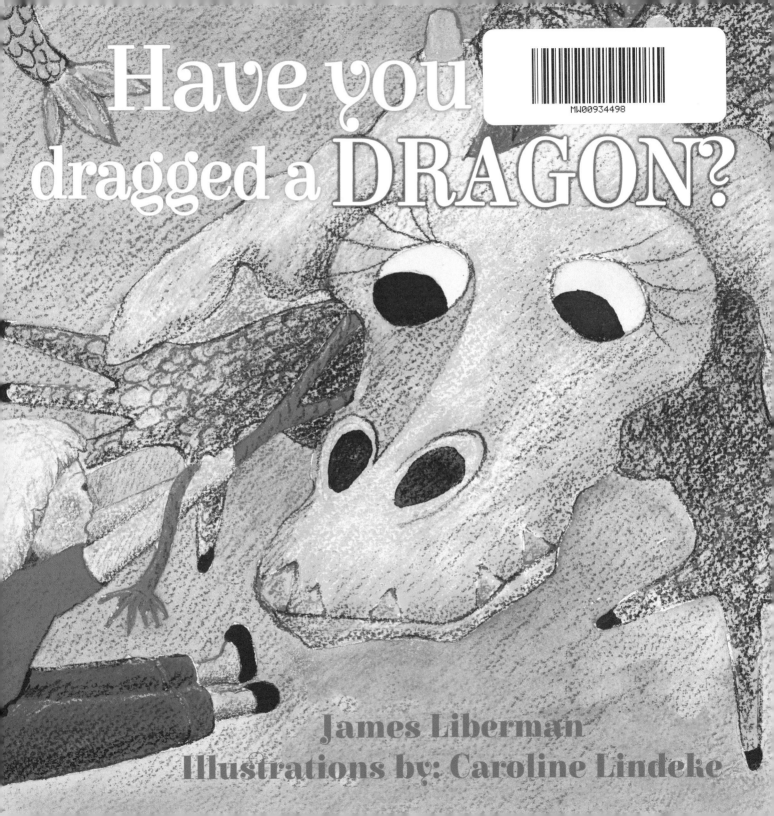

Have you dragged a DRAGON?

James Liberman

Illustrations by: Caroline Lindeke

SkyLight Books

Tandem Light Press
950 Herrington Rd.
Suite C128
Lawrenceville, GA 30044

Tandem Light Press paperback edition 2018

ISBN: 978-0-9992633-7-2
Library of Congress Control Number: 2018957968

PRINTED IN THE UNITED STATES OF AMERICA

Have you ever dragged a dragon

In a
Covered wagon

Across the **Wide** open **plains?**

I suppose you could be

Braggin'

About how your friendly Dragon

would keep you
sheltered from
the Rain.

and when it's
Sunny

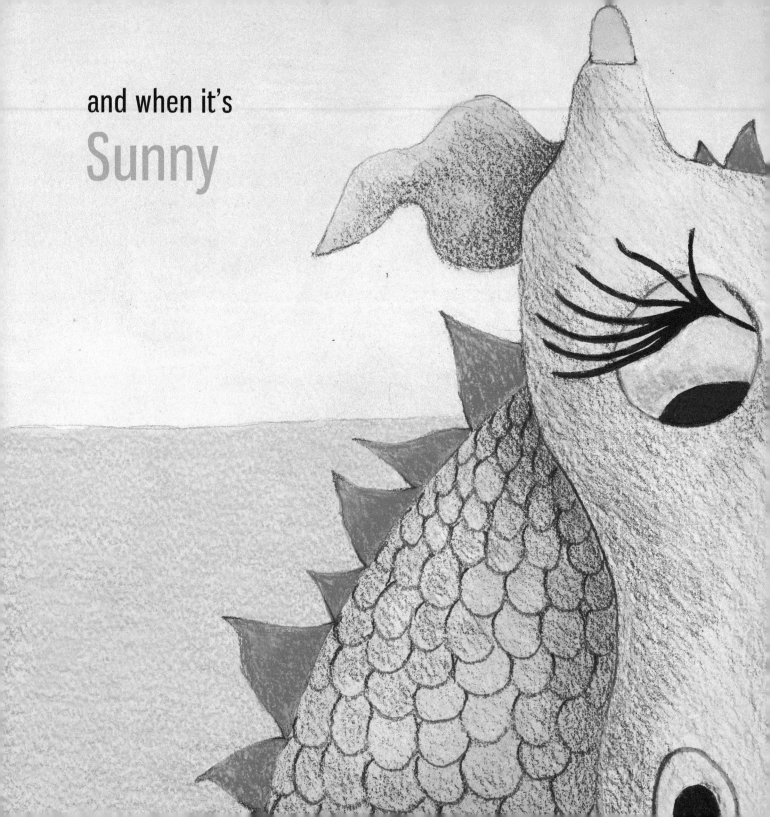

YOU and
dragon

can **play** a game of **tagg'n**

Romp **across** mesas

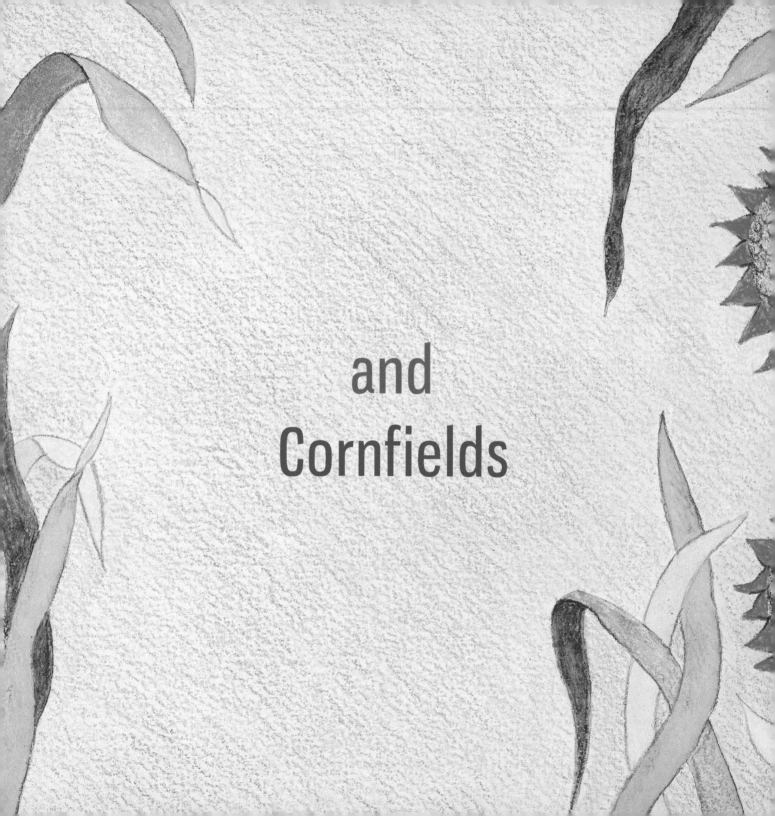

and
Cornfields

And when your day is done and you've had your

Dragon Fun

You'll be **draggin'** but your
Dragon

will **be**
Waggin' and
Waggin'

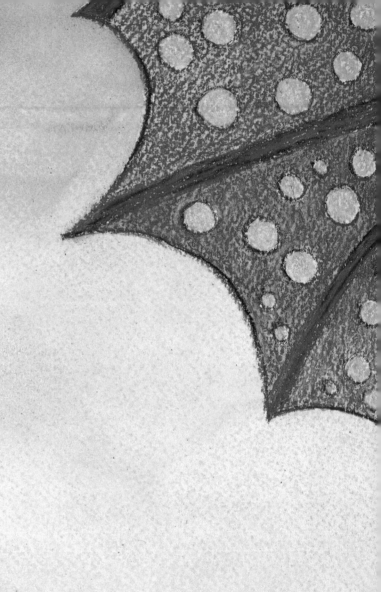

Then **Dragon**

will sit **up**

like a **Pup,**

Gather
you up,

Spread
out his tail and set sail;

Gently take you home

and **tuck** you into **Bed,**

And as you **close** your **Eyes,** Your Dragon

will surprise you with a kiss,

a somersault, a wink and a smile.

Have you ever dragged a dragon
In a covered wagon
Across the wide open plains?

I suppose you could be braggin'
About how your friendly dragon
Would keep you sheltered from the rain.

And when it's sunny you and dragon
Can play a game of tagg'n
Romp across mesas and corn fields

And when your day is done
And you've had your dragon fun
You'll be draggin' but your dragon
Will be waggin' and waggin'
And waggin his tail.

Then dragon will sit up like a pup,
Gather you up,
Spread out his tail and set sail;
Gently take you home
And tuck you into bed,

And as you close your eyes,
Your dragon will surprise you
With a kiss,
A somersault,
A wink,
And a smile.

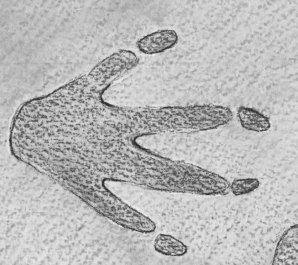

I've valued the encouragement of the entire Liberpeople clan, Peter and Paul Reynolds, and Caroline Lindeke, whose artistic whimsy captured the heart of my poem. Also, thanks to Caroline Smith and Tandem Light Press for bringing this book to fruition.

— JL

I am grateful to the following for their help and encouragement beginning with Jim Liberman for believing in me. Many thanks also go to Sally Santosuosso, Katy Wolff, Rob Wolff, Suzanne Jonsson, Ilse Plume, and Patsy Prior.

— CL

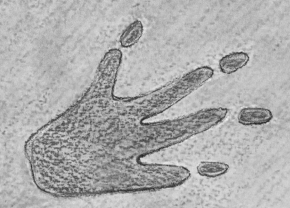

About the Author

James Liberman, a.k.a. Seamus O'Liberman, also answers to Jim. He enjoys tennis, tai chi, hiking, reading and dreaming.

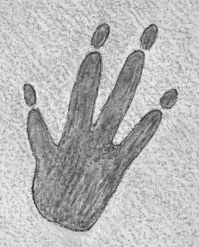

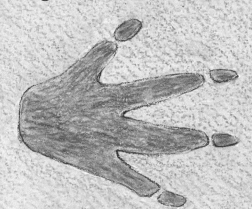

About the Illustrator

Caroline Lindeke is an artist/illustrator living in Cambridge, Massachusetts. She also teaches piano and enjoys yoga, tai chi, bike riding, and old movies.

Dedicated to Nelle, Julia, Chevy, Isaac, Louisa,
Ryan, Jet and Oz, and to all the kiddos young
and older.

- JL

To each of my grandchildren:
Cooper, Ella, Henry, Will, Ariana, Teddy,
Chester, Beckett, and Charlotte.

- CL

CPSIA information can be obtained
at www.ICGtesting.com
Printed in the USA
BVHW051016291119
565033BV00001B/1/P